On *Sesame Street,*
Gordon is played by Roscoe Orman,
and Susan by Loretta Long.

Copyright © 1990 Children's Television Workshop. Sesame Street puppet characters © 1990 Jim Henson Productions, Inc. All rights reserved under International and Pan-American Copyright Conventions. ® Sesame Street and the Sesame Street sign are trademarks and service marks of the Children's Television Workshop. Published in the United States by Random House, Inc., New York, and simultaneously in Canada by Random House of Canada Limited, Toronto, in conjunction with the Children's Television Workshop.

Library of Congress Cataloging-in-Publication Data
Hautzig, Deborah. Grover's bad dream / by Deborah Hautzig ; illustrated by Joe Mathieu. p. cm.—(A Sesame Street start-to-read book) "Random House/Children's Television Workshop." Summary: Grover feels neglected at Big Bird's birthday party when Big Bird gets everything his way.   ISBN 0-679-80898-1 (trade)   ISBN 0-679-90898-6 (lib. bdg.) [1. Puppets—Fiction. 2. Birthdays—Fiction.] I. Mathieu, Joseph, ill. II. Random House (Firm) III. Children's Television Workshop. IV. Title. V. Series: Sesame Street start-to-read books. PZ7.H2888 Gp 1990 [E]—dc20   90-32085 CIP AC

Manufactured in the United States of America   1 2 3 4 5 6 7 8 9 10

A Sesame Street Start-to-Read Book™

Grover's Bad Dream

by Deborah Hautzig

illustrated by Joe Mathieu

Random House/Children's Television Workshop

Grover wanted to find someone to play with. But everybody was busy. They were busy getting ready for Big Bird's birthday party.

Cookie Monster was busy making a cake.

Betty Lou was busy making a present.

Bert was busy cleaning up the house for the party.

Ernie was busy blowing up balloons.

So Grover went home.
"Nobody wants to play with me. They are all getting ready for Big Bird's birthday party."

Grover's mother said,
"Well, you have a nice gift for Big Bird.
Have you made a card yet?"
"No," said Grover.
"I will make one right now!"

Grover worked very hard.
"I hope Big Bird
will like my card," said Grover.
"Oh, he will!" said his mother.

Finally it was time
to go to the party.
Grover put on his favorite
shiny red jacket.
Then he went to
Ernie and Bert's house.

Everyone from Sesame Street was there.
Everyone but Big Bird!
"Shhh! Here he comes!" said Bert.
Ernie turned off the lights.
Big Bird came in.
"Gee, it's dark in here!" he said.

Ernie turned on the lights and everyone shouted, "SURPRISE!"

There were party hats for everyone.
"I get the crown,"
said Big Bird proudly.
"I'm the birthday bird!"

They played pin the tail on the cat.
Big Bird and Grover were the best.
"I won! I won!" shouted Big Bird.
"No, we both won," said Grover.
Betty Lou said,
"But it's Big Bird's birthday,
so he gets the prize!"

"Now it's time for birthday cake!" said Big Bird.
Everyone sang "Happy Birthday."
Then Big Bird blew out all the candles.
"You are getting so grown up," said Gordon. "Just think—five years old!"

"I am already SIX years old," Grover grumbled.
But nobody heard him.

Bert helped Big Bird cut the cake.
"That cake looks so good!"
said Grover.
He hoped he would get the piece
with the pink rose.

Big Bird said, "I get the first piece because it's MY birthday!"
He took the piece with the pink rose.

Everybody ate their cake.
Then Big Bird opened
his cards and presents.
"Gee, thanks, everybody!"
said Big Bird.

Ernie gave Big Bird a card.
"My cousin Fred made this card.
Isn't he a great artist?" said Ernie.
"Oh, YES!" said Big Bird.
Everyone admired the card.
"I made a card too!"
Grover said to himself.

At last the party was over,
and Grover went home.
"Did you have fun at the party?"
his mother asked.

"No," said Grover loudly.
"Big Bird got the crown,
and he said he won at
pin the tail on the cat,
but it was really a TIE—
and he got the piece of cake
with the pink rose
and he liked Ernie's cousin's card best.
It was a terrible, terrible party!"
Grover stomped off to his room.

That night Grover had a dream.
In the dream it was Grover's birthday!
Everybody was at the party—
everybody except Big Bird.

Grover blew out the candles
and got the first piece of cake.
It had a pink rose on it.
"Why does Grover get his cake first?"
asked Ernie.
"Because it is HIS birthday!"
said Bert.
Grover hugged his pillow.
What a nice dream this was!

Suddenly Big Bird came running into Grover's dream party. He had a blanket wrapped around him.

"Big Bird! Why are you wearing that blanket?" asked Grover.
"I LOST MY FEATHERS!" cried Big Bird.
"My beautiful yellow feathers are GONE! GONE! GONE!"

"Oh, NO!" cried Grover.
He yelled as loud as he could.
Grover's mother came running
into his room.
"Grover, wake up!" she said.
Grover did wake up.
Then he started to cry.
"Something awful happened!
It was my birthday
and there was a party,
but then Big Bird came,
and he lost all his feathers!
It was AWFUL!"
Grover howled.
"Oh my. You had a bad dream,"
said his mother.
She held him close.

Grover's mother made some hot cocoa.
"I had bad dreams sometimes
when I was a little girl," she said.
"You did?" asked Grover.
"Yes," said his mother.
"But then I woke up,
just the way you did."
"But," said Grover softly,
"do dreams come true?"
His mother held him in her lap.
"Nothing comes true
just because of a dream.
Things happen because of what you do
when you are awake —
not because of what you do in a dream."

The next morning Grover heard someone calling his name. He jumped out of bed and ran to the window. There was Big Bird!
"I came to thank you for the wonderful birthday card! It's my favorite!" called Big Bird.

Grover ran outside
and threw his arms around Big Bird.
"I am SO glad to see you!
And you have SO many
beautiful yellow feathers!"
Big Bird looked very surprised.
"Gee, sure I do. I'm a bird, you know,"
he said.

Grover laughed. "Yes, you are my favorite bird in the world!"
"Let's go play with my new birthday toys," said Big Bird. And that's just what they did.